Run for Fun

By Steve Metzger Illustrated by Jim Paillot

SCHOLASTIC INC.
New York Toronto London Auckland Sydney
Mexico City New Delhi Hong Kong Buenos Aires

Run to the blue hut.

Run with a big nut.

Run with a yellow tub.

Run like a bug.

Run with a bun.

Run and hum.

Run with a purple plum.

Run up and up.

Run and get your hair cut.

Run with a mutt.

Run for a bus.

Run with us.

Run for fun!

We like to run! Do you?